Donahon

This book belongs to:

~~DYLAN PORTER~~

_____

_____

First published 2004 by Walker Books Ltd
87 Vauxhall Walk, London SE11 5HJ

This edition produced 2004 for The Book People Ltd,
Hall Wood Avenue, Haydock, St Helens WA11 9UL

2 4 6 8 10 9 7 5 3 1

© 2004 Lucy Cousins
Illustrated in the style of Lucy Cousins by King Rollo Films Ltd

Lucy Cousins font © 2004 Lucy Cousins

"Maisy" audio visual series produced by King Rollo Films Ltd
for Universal Pictures International Visual Programming

Maisy™. Maisy is a registered trademark of Walker Books Ltd, London

Printed in China

British Library Cataloguing in Publication Data:
a catalogue record for this book is
available from the British Library

ISBN 1-84428-661-4

www.walkerbooks.co.uk

Maisy Goes Camping

Lucy Cousins

TED SMART

One summer afternoon, Maisy set off to go camping in the country.

Oh dear! The tent fell down.
They tried ... and tried ...

and tried again ... until
at last the tent stayed up.

What a big tent!
There's room for everyone.

After supper, they sang songs around the campfire. Then it was time for bed.

First in was Cyril, with his torch.
Nice pyjamas, Cyril!

One
in the
tent!

Next came Charley.
Mind the tent pegs, Charley!

Two in
the tent!

Then it was Tallulah's turn.
Sweet dreams, Tallulah!

Three in the tent!

And make room for Maisy...
Move up, everyone!

Four in the tent!

Is there room for one more? Come on, Eddie!

Oh dear!

Five in the...
(What a
squash!)

Five in the...
(What a
squeeze!)

Five in the... (What a squeezy squish-squash...)

Five in the tent!

Goodnight, campers!

POP!
Out popped
Cyril!

POP!
Out
popped
Tallulah!

Sleep tight, campers!

One in the tent...
Four under the stars...

And one in the tree.

Tuwoo!